THE
Fatal
SERIES COMPENDIUM

A SERIES SYNOPSIS AND LIST OF CHARACTERS

MARIE
NEW YORK TIMES BESTSELLING AUTHOR
FORCE

The Fatal Series Compendium
A series synopsis and list of characters
By: Marie Force
Published by HTJB, Inc.
Copyright 2025. HTJB, Inc.

Cover Design: Ashley Lopez
Print Layout: Champagne Book Design
Cover photography by Regina Wamba
Models: Robert John and Ellie Dulac

ISBN: 978-1958035-986

marieforce.com

The best way to stay in touch is to subscribe to my newsletter. Go to *marieforce.com* and subscribe in the box on the top of the screen that asks for your name and email. If you don't hear from me regularly, please check your spam filter and set up your email to allow my messages through to you so you never miss a new book, a chance to win great prizes or a possible appearance in your area.

The Fatal Series

Sam and Nick's story continues in an all-new blockbuster series that begins with STATE OF AFFAIRS!

From Marie:

As part of our celebration of FATAL AFFAIR's fifteenth anniversary, I'm so thrilled to bring you this Fatal Series Compendium, full of rich details about each book as well as a comprehensive list of the hundreds of characters who've appeared over the course of the sixteen-book and two-novella series. Pulling this together was a BEAST of a job, and I want to thank Gwen Neff for her help with the wrangling, Anne Woodall for proofing and the Fatal Series beta readers who also reviewed it: Kelly Hauhn, Amy Altieri, Gina Leveroni, Elizabeth Runyan, Viki Lawson, Jennifer Toman, Maricar Amit and Juliane Sullivan. We've done our best to capture the essence of each book, but please note that this section is FULL of spoilers. If you haven't read the entire series, proceed with caution! We've also done our best to get it right. I'm sure faithful readers will spot a few places where we missed, so please make sure to let me know if anything seems wrong to you.

For those of you who don't know the story behind the story, the Fatal Series was born from an article in the *Washington Post* around 2005 or 2006 that detailed the death of a congressman from Ohio, who'd been found at the bottom of his stairs by his chief of staff after he failed to show up for work. His death was initially considered suspicious. From that article came a question for me: who would have jurisdiction over the case? Would it be the FBI, the U.S. Capitol Police or the Metropolitan Police Department in Washington, D.C.? I did some research, found out it would be the MPD and took it from there. I ask myself all the time where this stuff comes from. I have no clue. I'm just glad it keeps on coming. Sam and Nick have been in my life so long, I should be preparing to send them off to college. They're as real to me as the people who live in my house (don't tell my family that), and I love them very much. I hope to continue writing them for many years to come.

I often get questions from readers asking which book something happened in, and to be honest, I'm sometimes not sure myself! Some of these books were written fifteen years ago or more, so the details become hazy for me to recite off the top of my head. I hope this compendium helps you find the info you're looking for, including when certain characters arrived on the scene, and to take a trip down memory lane with Sam, Nick and the rest of the Fatal cast.

Thank you to all the readers who have given this series— and the sequel series—such a remarkable run for all these years. Much more to come in Sam and Nick's ongoing story.

xoxo
Marie

THE
Fatal
SERIES COMPENDIUM

Fatal Series Prologue: One Night with You

Published: June 2, 2015

Back Cover Copy:

They were hot from the start…

Written for readers wondering about the "memorable" one-night stand between Sam Holland and Nick Cappuano that took place six years before *Fatal Affair* opens! Get all the details of Sam and Nick's unforgettable night together in this 14,000-word novella. You might want to keep a fan and some ice water handy, because this story is H-O-T!

More about the story...

After working a detail in the broiling sun all day, Metro Police Officer Samantha "Sam" Holland is dragged to a party on a Friday night by her sister Angela so she can meet up with a guy she likes named Spencer. While her sister flirts with Spencer on a deck somewhere in DC, Sam stands off to the side, watching a bunch of idiots get wasted while wishing she was at home in her pajamas.

When a drunk guy spills beer on Sam's skirt, Nick appears with a monogrammed handkerchief. After she's cleaned herself up, he asks if she wants to get out of there. They end up back at his place and spend the night together. Nick takes Sam home the next morning and promises to call her the minute he returns from a three-week work trip to Europe. She can't wait to see him again.

Characters

Recurring marked by **
**Samantha "Sam" Holland, Patrol Officer, daughter of Deputy Chief Skip Holland, Metro PD
**Nicholas "Nick" Domenic Cappuano, legislative aide to a U.S. Congress member

**Angela Holland, older sister to Sam
**Charles "Skip" Holland, father of Sam, Deputy Chief, Metro PD
**Jake Malone, Captain, Metro PD
**Leonard Stahl, Lieutenant, Metro PD

Spencer Radcliffe, Angela's love interest
Peter Gibson, Sam's platonic roommate, , future ex-husband, murdered in *Fatal Threat*
Dave Maxwell, Sam's platonic roommate
John Maxwell, Dave's brother

Book 1: Fatal Affair

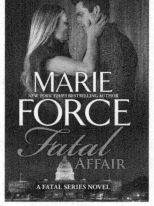

Published: June 20, 2010

Back Cover Copy:

D.C. Metro Police Detective Sergeant Sam Holland needs a big win to salvage her career—and her confidence—after a disastrous investigation led to tragedy. What she doesn't need is sparks flying with a former one-night stand, who also happens to be chief of staff to a dead U.S. Senator.

Senator John O'Connor is found brutally murdered in his bed, and Sam is assigned to the case. Things get complicated when Sam has to team up with Nick Cappuano, O'Connor's friend and chief of staff…and the man Sam had a memorable one-night stand with years earlier.

Their sexual chemistry still sizzles, and Sam has to fight to stay focused on the case. Sleeping with a material witness is another mistake she can't afford—especially when the bodies keep piling up.

More about the story...

Nick Cappuano can't believe his boss, U.S. Senator John O'Connor, is sleeping late on this of all days. The Senate is due to take up the landmark immigration bill that John has co-sponsored and wrestled to the floor for a vote. And he's oversleeping? Furious, Nick steps into his boss's apartment at the Watergate and finds him murdered in his bed.

Detective Sergeant Sam Holland, coming off a disastrous undercover investigation that ended with a dead child, is assigned to the case. When Sam walks into the Watergate apartment, she finds Nick, O'Connor's chief of staff and her one-night-stand from six years earlier. As she begins to investigate the senator's shocking murder, Sam learns that Nick did call her after that night, but her scheming roommate—now her ex-husband Peter Gibson—never gave her Nick's messages because he was interested in her. Everything they felt for each other that first night is still there, only Sam can't afford to indulge in her feelings for a witness when her career is on the line.

Sam's dad, Skip, is now a quadriplegic after being shot on the job two years earlier. His unsolved case haunts Sam and she works on it every chance she gets. He is cared for by Celia, his devoted nurse, and Sam finds out they were romantically involved before the shooting. As Sam and Nick spend more time together, piecing together the secrets of John's life, it becomes harder for her to resist the man she fell in love with six years ago and is apparently still in love with.

Nick delivers a stirring eulogy for John that puts him on the national map. Sam finds out she's been promoted to lieutenant, after the chief learns of the dyslexia she's kept hidden from her superiors. Nick is asked to take John's place in the Senate, and Sam arrests John's killer with Nick's help. Sam warns him that she'd be a terrible liability to him as a politician, but he's undeterred. He let her get away once before. He won't make that mistake a second time. He's purchased a townhome three doors down from her father's home on Ninth Street so she can help to care for Skip. John has left him a cabin in Leesburg that will allow him to remain a Virginia resident. They agree to give their relationship a shot.

Characters

Recurring marked by *

**Samantha "Sam" Holland, Detective Sergeant, Homicide Division, Metro PD
**Nicholas "Nick" Cappuano, Chief of Staff to Senator John O'Connor

Senator John Thomas O'Connor, D-VA, Nick's best friend and boss, murdered in *Fatal Affair*
**Joseph Farnsworth, Chief, Metro PD
**Christina Billings, Deputy Chief of Staff to Senator John O'Connor

**Trevor Donnelly, Communications Director for Senator John O'Connor

**Frederico "Freddie" Cruz, Detective, Homicide Division, Metro PD, Sam's partner

**Paul Conklin, Deputy Chief, Metro PD

Martin, Senator, Democrat, co-sponsor of John's bill

McDougal, Senate Majority Leader, Democrat

Carrie, Housekeeper for Graham and Laine O'Connor

**Graham O'Connor, former Senator from Virginia, father of John O'Connor

**Laine O'Connor, wife of Graham O'Connor, mother of John O'Connor

**Terry O'Connor, John O'Connor's troubled older brother

Lizbeth O'Connor Hamilton, sister of John O'Connor, wife of Royce, mother of Emma and Adam

Royce Hamilton, horse trainer, husband of Lizbeth, father of Emma and Adam

**William Stenhouse, Republican, Senate Minority Leader

**David Nelson, President of the United States, , deceased in *Fatal Fraud*

**Gloria Nelson, First Lady of the United States

**Celia, Skip's nurse and girlfriend

Marquise Johnson, drug dealer

Destiny Johnson, wife of Marquise Johnson, mother of Quentin

Quentin Johnson, infant son of Marquise and Destiny (Deceased before *Fatal Affair*)

**Dr. Lindsey McNamara, Chief Medical Examiner, Metro PD

Lucien Haverfield, O'Connor family attorney

**Dr. Anthony Trulo, Psychiatrist, Metro PD

Natalie St. Clair Jordan, ex-girlfriend of John O'Connor, married to Noel Jordan, murdered in *Fatal Affair*

Judson Knott, Chair, Virginia Democratic Party

Richard Manning, Vice Chair, Virginia Democratic Party

Patricia Donaldson, former girlfriend of John O'Connor, mother of Thomas O'Connor

Thomas John O'Connor, secret son of John O'Connor

**Tommy "Gonzo" Gonzales, Detective, Homicide Division, Metro PD

Noel Jordan, Deputy U.S. Attorney, husband of Natalie, murdered in *Fatal Affair*

Tara Davenport, Waitress who dated John O'Connor, murdered in *Fatal Affair*

**Elin Svendsen, Athletic Trainer at Total Fitness, former girlfriend of John O'Connor

Jimmy Chen, Client at Total Fitness

Robert O'Connor, brother to Graham, husband of Sally, father of Sarah, Thomas, Michael

Sally O'Connor, wife of Robert, mother of Sarah, Thomas, Michael

**Charity Miller, Assistant U.S. Attorney, Triplet

Severson, Patrol Officer, Arlington PD

**Arnold John "AJ" Arnold, Detective, Homicide Division, Metro PD, , murdered in *Fatal Frenzy*

**Matt O'Brien, Patrol Officer, Metro PD

**Higgins, Lieutenant, Explosive Division, Metro PD

**Jeannie McBride, Detective, Homicide Division, Metro PD

Andrea Daly, married mother with children, Terry O'Connor's alibi

**Darren Tabor, Reporter, *Washington Star*

Rico, Vendor, Eastern Market, friend to Sam

Brooke Hogan, niece of Sam, daughter of Tracy and Mike Hogan

Dawn Johnson, sister of Destiny Johnson

Tracy Holland Hogan, Sam's eldest sister, mother of Brooke, Abby and Ethan

Mike Hogan, Tracy's husband, father to Brooke, Abby and Ethan

Leo Cappuano, Nick's father, father of twin sons with Stacy

Stacy Cappuano, Leo's wife, father of twin sons with Leo

Angela Holland Radcliffe, Sam's older sister, mother of Jack

Spencer Radcliffe, Angela's husband

Faith Miller, Assistant U.S. Attorney, Triplet

Hope Miller Dobson, Assistant U.S. Attorney, Triplet

Cooper and Main, potential candidates for John's Senate seat

Book 2:
Fatal Justice

Published: January 3, 2011

Back cover copy:

Standing over the body of a Supreme Court nominee, Lieutenant Sam Holland is hip-deep in another high-profile murder case.

That she was one of the last people to see Julian Sinclair alive only complicates things even more. With her relationship with Senator Nick Cappuano heating up, they're attracting a lot of unwanted media attention and blinding flashbulbs. The pressure is on for Sam to find Sinclair's killer, but a new lead in her father's unsolved shooting puts her in unexpected danger. When long-buried secrets threaten to derail her relationship with Nick, Sam realizes that while

justice can be blind, mixing romance with politics has the
potential to be fatal.

More about the story...

On New Year's Eve, Sam takes the oath as a newly promoted lieutenant, in charge of the Homicide Division,
making an enemy of her displaced former commander
Leonard Stahl, who has been moved to Internal Affairs.
Next, Sam and Nick travel to the Capitol, where Nick is
sworn in as the new senator from Virginia.

Sam's team is called to a brutal homicide of a woman and
her children in the home of Clarence Reese, who's missing. Sam meets Nick's friend, Julian Sinclair, who's also
close with the O'Connors, when Julian comes to town as
a controversial Supreme Court nominee. Much to Sam
and Nick's dismay, the dashing new senator's relationship
with the homicide detective is the source of intense media
attention that intensifies when Sinclair is murdered.

Freddie returns to the gym where he met Elin during the
O'Connor investigation. He's hoping to lose his virginity
to the woman who spoke so freely about her sex life.

Standing over the body of a murdered Supreme Court
nominee Sam is hip-deep in another high-profile murder
case. The fact that she was one of the last people to see
Julian Sinclair alive complicates things even more.

Sam finds out Freddie has lied to her about why he didn't
answer his phone and sends him to Reese's house, thinking

Clarence might come back there. Freddie ends up getting shot. After meeting at Sam and Nick's New Year's Eve party, Gonzo begins dating Christina Billings. Nick decides to run for election to John's seat in the next election. He proposes to Sam in the Rose Garden of the White House during a state dinner. She accepts his proposal.

Characters

Recurring marked by **
Samantha "Sam" Holland, Lieutenant, Commander, Homicide Division, Metro PD
Nicholas "Nick" Cappuano, Junior Senator, Commonwealth of Virginia, U.S. Senate

Julian Sinclair, Supreme Court nominee, murdered in *Fatal Justice*
William Jeremiah, Supreme Court Justice, retired
Tom Hanigan, Chief of Staff to President David Nelson
Mike Zorn, Governor, Commonwealth of Virginia
Judy Zorn, First Lady, Commonwealth of Virginia
Clarence Reese, husband of Tiffany, father of Jorge, Ramon, Maria , all murdered or deceased *Fatal Justice*)
Hector Reese, brother of Clarence
Ginger, Legislative Aide to Senator Cappuano
Byron Riley, Chief Justice, U.S. Supreme Court
Robert "Bob" Cook, Senior Senator, Democrat, Commonwealth of Virginia, U.S. Senate
Harry Flynn, MD, Internist, friend of Nick's
William "Will" Tyrone, Detective, Homicide Division, Metro PD
Duncan Quick, Julian Sinclair's former partner

Ron Spaulding, assaulted Duncan Quick

Preston Sinclair, brother of Julian Sinclair, History Professor, Catholic University (Deceased *Fatal Justice*)

Diandra Sinclair, wife of Preston, conservative commentator

**Devon Sinclair, attorney, son of Preston and Diandra, nephew to Julian

Austin Sinclair, accountant, son of Preston and Diandra, nephew to Julian

Robert "Junior" Desposito, federal prisoner

**Juliette Cruz, mother of Freddie

Tucker Farrell, chef, partner of Devon Sinclair, murdered in *Fatal Justice*

**Andrews, Captain, Explosives Division, Metro PD

Tony Sanducci, abortion protestor

Cynthia "Cindy" Kaine, abortion protestor

Mac Healy, pizza delivery man

**Peterson, Patrol Officer, Metro PD

Trip Ackerman, Chair, Senate Judiciary Committee

Montgomery, Police Officer, Metro PD

**Andrew "Andy" Simone, Attorney, friend of Nick's, husband of Elsa

Mike, White House Valet

Book 3:
Fatal
Consequences

Published: July 18, 2011

Back cover copy:

*The murder of two members of the Capitol Cleaning Service
might've been just another homicide investigation if one
of them hadn't been romantically involved with a married
senator from Arizona.*

Lt. Sam Holland and her team are plunged into another
complex case that at first seems routine. But as Sam tugs on
the threads of the investigation she uncovers a deep, dark
Washington secret that threatens the careers of some of the
government's highest-ranking officials. Racing to catch a

killer before he can strike again, Sam and her fiancé, U.S. Senator Nick Cappuano, attempt to plan a wedding while her colleague Detective Tommy "Gonzo" Gonzales faces life-changing news.

More about the story...

At Celia and Skip's Valentine's Day wedding, Nick receives a phone call from his colleague, Senator Henry Lightfeather of Arizona, who has found an employee of the Capitol Cleaning Services, dead in her apartment. Sam and her team are plunged into an investigation that leads to the highest seats of power in the United States government as she tries to plan a wedding with the hottest politician in the country. Wedding planner extraordinaire, Shelby Faircloth, comes to their rescue and quickly becomes a valued new friend to DC's latest power couple.

After a stint in rehab, Terry O'Connor becomes Nick's chief of staff. Detective Jeannie McBride is kidnapped, held hostage and sexually assaulted. After a frantic search, Jeannie is found traumatized and badly injured with a message for Sam: back off the investigation into the dead women or you will be next.

Gonzo learns he fathered a son with a former girlfriend and sets out to find him and bring him into his life.

On a campaign stop at a home for children in Richmond, Nick meets Scotty Dunlap and is immediately captivated by the charming young boy who came to live at the home after the deaths of his mother and grandfather. After their visit, Nick sends Scotty a David Ortiz jersey in honor of Scotty's favorite member of the Boston Red Sox, the team they both love. Nick can't stop thinking about the amazing boy and starts to wonder if he and Sam could give him a loving home.

Sam's dangerous ex-husband Peter Gibson is released from jail on a technicality, shocking Sam and her team. Nick gives his deadbeat mother twenty thousand dollars. Gonzo gets custody of his son, and his girlfriend, Christina, vows to be there for them both. Sam suffers a miscarriage as she arrests a killer. When Senator Cook is forced to resign after being caught up in a scandal, Nick becomes the senior senator from Virginia, weeks after being sworn into office.

Characters

Recurring Indicated with **
**Lieutenant Samantha "Sam" Holland, Commander, Homicide Division, Metro PD
**Senator Nicholas "Nick" Cappuano, Junior Senator, Commonwealth of Virginia, U.S. Senate

Henry Lightfeather, D-AZ, U.S. Senate
Regina Argueta de Castro, Capitol Cleaning Service, murdered in *Fatal Consequences*
**Lori Phillips, mother of Gonzo's son, , murdered in *Fatal Scandal*
**Alejandro "Alex" Gonzales, infant son of Tommy Gonzales and Lori Phillips
Rex Connolly, Lori's boyfriend
Annette Lightfeather, Henry's wife

Tony, Nick's driver

**Irene Littlefield, director of the state home for children in Richmond

**Scotty Dunlap, twelve-year-old ward of the state whom Nick befriends

Mr. Sanchez, Scotty's former math teacher

JoAnn Smithson, owner, Capitol Cleaning Service

Maria Espanosa, employee, Capital Cleaning Service, murdered in *Fatal Consequences*

**Tom Forrester, U.S. Attorney

Seamus O'Grady, cook, former husband of Regina Argueta de Castro

Debbie Hopkins, upstairs neighbor of Maria Espanosa

Selina Rameriz, employee, Capital Cleaning Service

Mark Angelo, Gonzo's friend, introduced him to Lori

**Shelby Faircloth, wedding planner in Georgetown

Tornquist, former Senator, Republican from Oregon, U.S. Senator

Trent, Senator, Republican from Oregon, U.S. Senate

Lewis, Senator, Republican, U.S. Senate

**Michael Wilkinson, boyfriend of Detective Jeannie McBride

**Nicoletta Bernadino, mother to Nick Cappuano

Leon Morton, Judge, Family Court, presides over Gonzo's custody hearing

Justine Avery Tavers, Social Worker, overseeing Alex's case

**"Archie" Archelotta, Lieutenant, Commander, IT Division, Metro PD

Bradford Tillinghast, Lobbyist, Tillinghast & Young

Jackson, Patrol Officer, Metro PD

Gerald Price, owner of the home rented by Clarence Reese

Jack Bartholomew, Chief of Staff to Vice President Joseph Gooding

**Joseph Gooding, Vice President of the United States

Daniels, Speaker of the House of Representatives

Grayson, Captain, Metro Fire Department

Craig Lowry, contractor hired by Nick to install ramp on Ninth Street

Mitchell Sanborn, Chair, Democratic National Committee, deceased in *Fatal Frenzy*

Dr. Maggie Tyndall, OB/GYN, dating Harry Flynn

Cheri Anderson, Administrative Assistant

Book 3.5:
Fatal Destiny
A Fatal
Series Wedding
Novella

Published: September 5, 2011

Back cover copy:

With the week of their wedding finally upon them, Washington, D.C., Police Lieutenant Sam Holland and her fiancé, Senator Nick Cappuano, are at odds. In the aftermath of a tragic loss, they struggle to reconnect as the big day draws near and their work keeps pulling them apart. When a new clue in a cold case resurfaces, Nick asks Sam not to take any foolish chances before the wedding and to leave it alone for the time being. Sam agrees, but she can't let it go entirely and winds up trapped in an explosive situation. Then an unwelcome visitor from her past threatens her future happiness. With trouble at every turn, will Sam survive long enough to walk down the aisle?

More about the story...

With one week until Sam and Nick say, 'I do,' Sam is still grieving over her recent miscarriage and is convinced she can't endure the risk of another pregnancy, so she sees their friend Harry about birth control. Nick knows something is wrong and wonders if Sam is having second thoughts about the wedding. Sam makes a promise to Nick before the wedding to put her safety ahead of everything else and ends up with another concussion after being shot at. Nick's protective instincts save Sam when her ex-husband Peter tries to kill her again. Nick's deadbeat mother, Nicoletta, tries to crash the wedding, where Nick has arranged for Sam's favorite singer, Jon Bon Jovi, to sing the song for their first dance.

Characters

Recurring Indicated with **
**Samantha "Sam" Holland, Lieutenant, Commander, Homicide Division, Metro PD
**Nicholas "Nick" Cappuano, Senior Senator, Commonwealth of Virginia, U.S. Senate

Trace Simmons, gangbanger
Darius Gardner, gangbanger

**Roberto Castro, Sam's longtime informant
**Angel, Roberto's girlfriend
**Ramsey, Detective Sergeant, Special Victims Division, Metro PD
Leticia Nixon, Daycare Worker
**Derek Kavanaugh, Deputy Chief of Staff to President David Nelson, longtime friend of Nick's
**Victoria Kavanaugh, Derek's wife, , murdered in *Fatal Deception*

Book 4: Fatal Flaw

Published: July 1, 2012

Back cover copy:

Back from their honeymoon, Senator Nick Cappuano and D.C. Police Lieutenant Sam Holland are ready for some normalcy after the whirlwind of their wedding, but someone has other plans for them.

When Sam discovers wedding cards containing thinly veiled death threats, she's not sure if she or Nick is the target. Already on edge, Sam and her team start investigating a series of baffling murders. The victims are well-liked with no known enemies, and the murders are carried out in a clean and efficient manner. Unable to find a clear motive for the deaths, Sam feels like she's chasing her tail. With no obvious connection between the victims, Sam soon suspects that she may be the ultimate prize in the killer's clever game. When the danger starts to hit a little too close to home, she has two goals: find the elusive murderer and manage to live long enough to enjoy her happily ever after.

More about the story…

Sam and Nick return from their Bora Bora honeymoon, and minutes after she's back on the clock she's called to a puzzling crime scene. As the bodies start to pile up, the case becomes more baffling. The victims were well liked, and there's no sign of robbery. After the third similar crime where the victims didn't seem to have any enemies, it's clear they must be connected but the team cannot figure out how.

Sam and Nick receive threatening notes mixed in with wedding cards they receive at both their offices. Freddie and Elin reach a crossroad in their relationship. Terry O'Connor and Lindsey McNamara consider taking the next step in their romance. Sam and Nick decide to be foster parents to Scotty. Jeannie and Michael try to find a new normal following her assault. Skip Holland has a serious case of pneumonia that has Sam wanting to clean up his one unresolved case. Nick takes Scotty to Boston to see the Red Sox.

Characters

Recurring Marked with **
**Samantha "Sam" Holland Cappuano, Lieutenant, Commander, Homicide Division, Metro PD

Nicholas "Nick" Cappuano, Senior Senator, Commonwealth of Virginia, U.S. Senate

Carl Olivio, owner of Carl's restaurant, murdered in *Fatal Flaw*

Daniel Alvarez, worked at Carl's, murdered in *Fatal Flaw*

Joseph Alvarez, father of Daniel

Gentile, Patrol Officer, Metro PD

Steven Coyne, Skip's first partner, murdered on the job years ago, case unsolved

Alice Coyne Fitzgerald, widow of Steven, remarried

Tyler Fitzgerald, son of Alice Fitzgerald, died years earlier under suspicious circumstances

Caleb Fitzgerald, son of Alice Fitzgerald

Cameron Fitzgerald, son of Alice Fitzgerald

Tremont, Captain, Chief of Detectives, Metro PD

Crystal Martin Trainer, mother, murdered in *Fatal Flaw*

Nicole Trainer, daughter of Crystal

Josh Trainer, son of Crystal

Jed Trainer, husband of Crystal

Janet Nelson, works at consulting firm, was having affair with Jed Trainer

Leroy Augustine, lead in Skip's case, deceased in *Fatal Flaw*

Mrs. Nesbitt, Principal, Alice Deal Middle School

Donna Kasperian, Crystal Trainer's best friend

Dr. Taylor Kingsley, marriage counselor to Jed and Crystal Trainer

Hernandez, Captain, Patrol Division, Metro PD

St. James, Officer, Metro PD

Raymond Jefferies, retired teacher, murdered in *Fatal Flaw*

Sabrina Jefferies Campion, daughter of Raymond Jefferies

**Dr. Byron Tomlinson, Deputy Medical Examiner, Metro PD

Huff, Patrol Officer, Metro PD

**Mr. Cruz, father of Freddie, husband of Juliette

James Lynch, lawyer, murdered in *Fatal Flaw*

Amanda Lynch, wife of James

Dr. Norman Morganthau, former Chief Medical Examiner, Metro PD

**Avery Hill, Special Agent-in-Charge, Criminal Investigative Division, Federal Bureau of Investigation

Melissa Morgan Woodmansee, ex-friend of Sam's

Justin Woodmansee, Melissa's ex-husband

Debbie Donahue, mutual friend of Sam and Melissa

Sean Morgan, father of Melissa, murdered in *Fatal Flaw*

Frieda Morgan, mother of Melissa, murdered in *Fatal Flaw*

Book 5: Fatal Deception

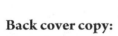

Published: November 12, 2012

Back cover copy:

The wife of the White House deputy chief of staff has been beaten to death, and their one-year-old daughter is missing.

D.C. Police Lieutenant Sam Holland is in charge of the murder investigation, but she's forced to collaborate with Special Victims Unit detectives as well as thorn-in-her-side FBI Special Agent Avery Hill. Then, a cold case of her father's resurrects old hurts—a distraction Sam cannot afford. As Sam's investigation heats up, so does Nick's political career—and the heat carries over to their bedroom. Will Sam put the pieces together in time to catch a killer and find the baby, or will ambition, greed and lies prove fatal?

More about the story...

Derek Kavanaugh, Deputy Chief of Staff to the President, has come home from a weekend retreat at Camp David to find his wife, Victoria, beaten to death in their kitchen and his one-year-old daughter, Maeve, missing. Lieutenant Sam Holland is put in charge of the case and forced to collaborate with Special Victims Unit detectives and FBI Special Agent Avery Hill. The investigation uncovers a nefarious political plot that has Derek questioning everything he thought he knew about his wife and his marriage as the frantic search for Maeve continues.

A cold case of her father's leads Sam to suspend Jeannie and Will for lying to her, even though they thought it was what she'd want to protect her dad's reputation. Jeannie and Michael get engaged. Nick's political career heats up and he's asked to deliver the keynote speech at the Democratic National Convention.

Sam is injured when she walks into a robbery in progress in a convenience store. Scotty will stay with Nick and Sam while he attends a baseball camp. All of them hope that this will be a permanent arrangement. Knowing they will need help if they take in Scotty, Nick and Sam hire Shelby to run their lives.

Characters

Recurring Marked with **
** Samantha "Sam" Holland Cappuano, Lieutenant, Commander, Homicide Division, Metro PD
**Nicholas "Nick" Cappuano, Senior Senator, Commonwealth of Virginia, U.S. Senate

**Maeve Kavanaugh, one-year-old daughter of Derek and Victoria, missing in *Fatal Deception*
**Harper, Detective, Special Victims Unit, Metro PD
Felicity Rider, Legal Aide for Senator Stenhouse
**Kevin Kavanaugh, Agent, Drug Enforcement Administration (DEA), brother of Derek
**Dr. Rob Anderson, Emergency Medicine, George Washington University Hospital
Denise Desposito, died six years earlier, name used in fraud, daughter of William Eldridge
William Eldridge, father of Denise Desposito, Officer, Patterson Financial Group, (deceased)
Dr. Simsbury, Plastic Surgeon, George Washington University Hospital
Susan Jacobson, Managing Partner, Callahan Rice, Victoria's former firm
Brandon Halliwell, Chairman, Democratic National Committee
**Arnold "Arnie" Patterson, Independent candidate for President
Dominic Rafael, Republican candidate for President
Ginger Dickenson, stay-at-home mother to Trevor, friend of Victoria
Bertha Ray, babysitter

Bobby Ray, son of Bertha, murdered in *Fatal Deception*
Patrice, ex-girlfriend of Nick's
Wilkins and Ramirez, Patrol Officers, Metro PD
**Giselle "Gigi" Dominguez, Detective, Homicide Division, Metro PD
**Dani Carlucci, Detective, Homicide Division, Metro PD
Roy Tornquist, Independent, Congressman from Ohio, U.S. House of Representatives
**Jessica Townsend, Chief Counsel, Metro PD
Christian Patterson, Senior Adviser for father, Arnie Patterson, VP in Patterson Financial
Colton Patterson, Senior Adviser for father, Arnie Patterson
Sam, receptionist, Patterson Campaign Headquarters
Porter Gillespie, aide to Colton Patterson
Jonathon Thayer, aide to Christian Patterson
Jerry Smith, driver, odd jobs, Patterson family
Dr. Bernard Saltzman, OB/GYN, Washington Hospital Center
Dupont, Patrol Officer, Metro PD
**Ella Holland Radcliffe, infant daughter of Angela and Spencer, niece to Sam, named for Sam and Angela's grandmother
**Beckett, Patrol Officer, Metro PD
**Brenda Ross, mother to Sam, Angela and Tracy Holland, ex-wife of Skip
Marcella, Assistant to Director Hamilton, Federal Bureau of Investigation
**Troy Hamilton, Director, Federal Bureau of Investigation, murdered in *Fatal Identity*

Book 6: Fatal Mistake

Published: June 17, 2013

Back cover copy:

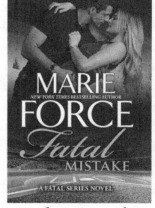

A critical error. A Cinderella season cut short. A star player murdered.

D.C. is recovering from angry riots after one player's mistake blew the D.C. Federals' chance at the World Series, and Lt. Sam Holland is determined to unravel the twisted web of motives behind the star center fielder's death. Was it a disgruntled fan, a spurned lover or a furious teammate? While Sam digs through clues, her husband, U.S. Senator Nick Cappuano, fights for his political life in the final days of his reelection campaign as financial irregularities threaten his future. It's a distraction Nick can ill afford with Sam in the midst of another high-profile murder investigation and both of them trying to help their adopted son, Scotty, cope with the murder of a ball player he admired. Determined to bring the killer to justice, Sam must root out the truth before another mistake proves fatal.

More about the story...

When D.C. Feds star center fielder Willie Vasquez drops a fly ball he should've easily caught, the team's chance to make the World Series is blown. The city descends into riots. When the dust settles, Willie is found murdered in a dumpster behind the Smithsonian, setting off a new investigation for Lieutenant Holland and her team. Scotty is despondent over the murder of a player he met at his recent camp.

Sam is determined to unravel the twisted web of motives behind the star center fielder's death while Nick fights for his political life in the final days of his Senate reelection campaign as financial irregularities threaten his future.

FBI Agent Avery Hill is brought in on the case as he is friend with the D.C. Feds owner. A sex trafficking ring is uncovered during the investigation. Lieutenant Stahl is fired after it's proven that he has been leaking information to the press. He attacks Sam at home while Nick is in Iran.

Characters

Recurring Marked with **
** Samantha "Sam" Holland Cappuano, Lieutenant, Commander, Homicide Division, Metro PD

**Nicholas "Nick" Cappuano, Senior Senator, Commonwealth of Virginia, U.S. Senate

Willie Vasquez, Center Fielder, D.C. Feds, murdered in *Fatal Mistake*

Rick Lind, star pitcher, D.C. Feds, murdered in *Fatal Mistake*

Carla Lind, Rick's wife

Carmen Peña Vásquez, wife of Willie, mother of Miguel and Jose

Bob Minor, Coach, D.C. Feds

Cecil Mulroney, Right Fielder, D.C. Feds

Eric Douglas, Agent, U.S. Secret Service

Ray Jestings, Owner, D.C. Federals

Elle Kopelsman Jestings, Owner, Washington *Star* and D.C. Federals

Aaron, Assistant to Ray Jestings

Jamie Clark, Athletic Trainer, D.C. Feds

Garrett Collins, General Manager, D.C. Feds

Hugh Bixby, Director of Security, D.C. Feds

James "Jim" Settle, General Manager, WFBR-FM radio station

Ben "Big Ben" Markinson, On-Air Personality, WFBR-FM radio station

Marcy, Producer, Big Ben Show, WFBR-FM radio station

Jim Morris, Security, D.C. Feds

Kyle Davidson, Security, D.C. Feds

**George Terrell, Deputy to Special Agent-in-Charge Avery Hill, Federal Bureau of Investigation

Eduardo Peña, brother of Carmen Vasquez

Boris, security for Elle Koplesman

Horace, security for Elle Koplesman

George McPhearson, Sports Agent to Willie Vasquez
Chris Ortiz, Player, D.C. Feds
Charlie Engal, Manager, Willie Vasquez
Nathan Cleary, bully to Scotty
Toni, Agent, U.S. Secret Service
Brice, Agent, U.S. Secret Service
Dr. Leonard, Team Physician, D.C. Feds
**Max Haggerty, Lieutenant, Crime Scene Investigation Division, Metro PD
Ramon Perez, Player, D.C. Feds
Liza Benjamin, Friend to Jamie Clark
Sarah "Ginger" Moreland, human trafficking victim
Amber Tattorelli, human trafficking victim
Deanna Moreland, Sarah's mother
Bruce Jones, Manager, Capitol Motor Inn
**Erica Lucas, Detective, Special Victims Unit, Metro PD
Tim Russo, Attorney

Book 7:
Fatal Jeopardy

Published: March 24, 2014

Back cover copy:

Washington, D.C. Police Lieutenant Sam Holland and her husband, U.S. Senator Nick Cappuano, have been looking forward to a quiet Thanksgiving with their son.

But any thoughts of a restful holiday are dashed when Sam and Nick return home to a gruesome scene: her seventeen-year-old niece Brooke, barely conscious and covered in blood on their front stoop. With lines between personal and professional blurring in this emotionally charged, deeply personal case, Sam is relying on Nick more than ever for support. But when suspicious images from the night in question appear on social media, Sam begins to wonder if her niece is telling her everything she knows about what really happened. And when Nick questions her tactics—and her ethics—as she races against the clock, Sam will need to decide how far she's willing to go to prove Brooke is a victim, not a murderer.

More about the story…

Sam and Nick are counting down to vacation when she is catapulted into another case involving her niece Brooke and a group of teenagers found murdered in the home of a prominent DC resident. Brooke is seriously hurt and dumped on Sam and Nick's doorstep. At the same time Gonzo, Freddie and the rest of the Homicide squad are investigating a mass murder that involved teenagers, drinking and drugs that ended in murder.

Nick is upset with Sam as the investigation has prevented them from disconnecting from the world to relieve the stress of the last few months as they had hoped to do. Nick has his own career to consider when President Nelson informs him that Vice President Gooding will step down to battle a brain tumor. Nelson would like Nick to replace Gooding as Vice President.

Gonzo gets full custody of his son Alex and is then shot during a confrontation at the Springer home. Skip has risky surgery to remove the bullet lodged in his spine. Nick accepts Nelson's offer and becomes Vice President, even though he and Sam have significant reservations.

Characters

Recurring Marked with **
** Samantha "Sam" Holland Cappuano, Lieutenant, Commander, Homicide Division, Metro PD
**Nicholas "Nick" Cappuano, Senior Senator, Commonwealth of Virginia, U.S. Senate, becomes Vice President in *Fatal Jeopardy*

Hugo Springer, teenager, murdered in *Fatal Jeopardy*
William "Billy" Springer Jr., brother to Hugo, killed by police in *Fatal Jeopardy*
William "Bill" Springer, prominent lawyer, husband of Marissa, father of Hugo and Billy, found dead in *Fatal Jeopardy*
**Marissa Springer, wife of Bill, mother of Hugo and Billy
Michael Chastain, teenager, murdered in *Fatal Jeopardy*
Edna Chen, housekeeper for Springers, murdered in *Fatal Jeopardy*
Todd Braden, teenager, murdered in *Fatal Jeopardy*
Kevin Corrigan, teenager, murdered in *Fatal Jeopardy*
Lacey Morrison, teenager, murdered in *Fatal Jeopardy*
Kelsey Lewis, teenager, murdered in *Fatal Jeopardy*
Julia Pelse, teenager, murdered in *Fatal Jeopardy*
Shana Gilford, teenager, murdered in *Fatal Jeopardy*
Maura McHugh, teenager, murdered in *Fatal Jeopardy*
Gideon Young, Headmaster, Remington School for Girls
Linda, Receptionist, Remington School for Girls
Sebastian Ryder, Director of Security, Remington School for Girls
Trent, Security, Remington School for Girls
Dr. Kelison, Therapist, Remington School for Girls

Mr. Galbraith, Principal, Wilson High School
Hoda Danziger, teen, friend of Brooke's
Brody Mitchell, teen
Adam Braden, adoptive father of Todd
Sarah Braden, adoptive mother of Todd
Davey, teen
Tyler Barnes, teen
Jeff Barnes, Tyler's father
Pauline Barnes, Tyler's mother
Nico, Hoda's boyfriend
**Ambrose Pierce, Director, U.S. Secret Service
Justin, teen
**Roback, Captain, Vice Division, Metro PD
**Cole McDonald, Lieutenant, Vice Division, Metro PD
Richard Clayborne, Speaker of the House, U.S. House of
Representatives

Book 8:
Fatal Scandal

Published: January 13, 2015

Back cover copy:

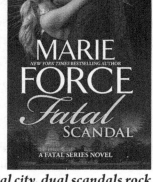

As a new year dawns in the capital city, dual scandals rock the Metropolitan Police Department—and Lieutenant Sam Holland is right in the middle of them.

Chief Farnsworth is catching heat for the way he handled a recent homicide investigation, and Detective Gonzales is accused of failing to disclose an earlier connection to the judge who decided his custody hearing. When Gonzo's fight for his child turns deadly and he has a shaky alibi, Sam must defend *two* of her closest colleagues. All while her husband, Vice President Nick Cappuano, settles into his new office at the White House. Nick begins to wonder if the president is using him for a political boost, and his worries mount over a complication in the plans to adopt Scotty at a time when Sam is being put through the wringer by the always-rabid D.C. press corps. As the evidence against Gonzo piles up, Sam suspects someone is gunning for her—and her team.

More about the story...

The new year brings new drama for Lieutenant Sam Holland and Vice President Nick Cappuano. Two scandals rock the Metro Police Department: Chief Farnsworth is catching heat for the way he handled the Springer homicide investigation, and Gonzo is accused of failing to disclose an earlier connection to the judge who decided his custody hearing.

Alex's mother, Lori, is found murdered and Gonzo is a suspect.

Vice President Nick Cappuano settles into his new office at the White House and life in the gilded cage is not all it's cracked up to be.

A complication in the plan to adopt Scotty arises. Shelby discovers that she's pregnant, and when she learns of Avery's infatuation with Sam, she is deeply hurt. Elin is attacked at the gym, which turns out to be a decoy to get Freddie away from Sam. Sam speaks to Lilia Van Nostrand, her Second Lady Chief of Staff.

Marissa Springer and disgraced Lieutenant Stahl take Sam hostage in the Springer basement. He wraps her in razor wire and threatens to set her on fire. Sam thinks only of Nick, Scotty and her family in what may be her final minutes.

Scotty meets his biological father, the last hurdle to Sam and Nick adopting him.

Characters

Recurring Marked with **
** **Samantha "Sam" Holland Cappuano,** Lieutenant, Commander, Homicide Division, Metro PD
****Nicholas "Nick" Cappuano,** Vice President of the United States

****John "Brant" Brantley Jr.,** Lead Agent for Vice President Cappuano, U.S. Secret Service
****Melinda,** Agent on Vice President Cappuano's detail, U.S. Secret Service, called Secret Service Barbie by Sam
****Darcy,** Agent, U.S. Secret Service
George Phillips, brother of Lori
Tony, Super, Gonzo's apartment building
Davidson, Lieutenant, Commander, Special Victims Unit, Metro PD
****Helen,** Administrative Assistant to Chief Joe Farnsworth, Metro PD
****Norris,** Captain, Commander, Public Affairs Division, Metro PD
Sara Angelo, Lori Phillips's best friend
Carson Billings, Criminal Defense Attorney, brother of Christina Billings
Liam Hughes, met Lori online
Andre Elliott, former member of gym where Elin works

Delany, Sergeant in Booking, Metro PD
**Debra Nixon, Lead Agent for Scotty Dunlap, U.S. Secret Service
Monica Taylor, Reporter, Good Morning, CBC
Pamela Desjardens, Assistant to Bill Springer
James Donlon, Private Investigator
Destiny, Receptionist to James Donlon
Lauren, Receptionist to Vice President Cappuano
**Nickleson, Captain, Commander, SWAT Division, Metro PD
**Tony D'Alessandro, Waiter, Biological father of Scotty Dunlap Cappuano
Jeffrey, Steward, *Air Force Two*

Book 9:
Fatal Frenzy

Published: September 15, 2015

Back cover copy:

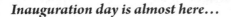

Inauguration day is almost here...

Lieutenant Sam Holland is on medical leave, recovering from an attack that shook her to the core. With no case to distract her, she's trying to stay busy—even voluntarily meeting with her new White House staff. But it's not enough to keep the horrific memories at bay, and her family is worried, especially her husband, Vice President Nick Cappuano. Nick is dealing with his own demons where his wife's safety is concerned, losing night after night of sleep as he takes steps to ensure what happened that day will never happen again. The pressure is building inside the

Cappuanos' marriage, and something's got to give before Nick takes the oath of office. A series of knife attacks in the midst of inauguration madness has the District on edge, and when the case strikes shockingly close to home, Sam returns to help hunt down a heartless killer. In a case full of ugly twists and turns, Sam will have to confront her past and find her strength again…before it's too late.

More about the story…

Lieutenant Sam Holland is on medical leave, recovering from the attack perpetrated by disgraced former Lieutenant Stahl and Marissa Springer. Sam's trying to figure out what her new purpose in life is as she recovers from her injuries. She tries to stay busy—even voluntarily meeting with her new White House staff—so she won't think about being being wrapped in razor wire and threatened with fire. Nick is dealing worries about how to keep her safe.

Gonzo leads the knife attack investigation, during which his partner, Detective AJ Arnold, is shot and killed in the line of the duty. Sam is off duty and out of touch when Arnold is killed, but his murder brings her back to work.

On Inauguration Day, Nick is sworn in as Vice President. Sam punches Detective Ramsey for suggesting she got what she deserved from Stahl. He falls backward down the stairs and breaks his wrist and suffers a concussion. Sam may face assault charges.

Freddie gets suspended for beating up the guy who attacked Elin. While he is suspended, he and Elin get engaged.

Scotty's adoption is finalized. He is now Scotty Dunlap Cappuano.

Characters

Recurring Marked with **
** Samantha "Sam" Holland Cappuano, Lieutenant, Commander, Homicide Division, Metro PD
**Nicholas "Nick" Cappuano, Vice President of the United States

Wilson, Lieutenant, Commander Internal Affairs Division, Metro PD
William Enright, Associate at Griffen + Smoltz, one of the stabbing victims who survived in *Fatal Frenzy*
Andrea, Director of Communications, Office of the Second Lady
Mackenzie, Director of Schedule and Travel, Office of the Second Lady
Keira, Policy Specialist, Office of the Second Lady
Simon Griffen, Managing Partner, Griffen + Smoltz
Sid Androzzi (a/k/a Giuseppe Besozzi) one of FBI's Ten Most Wanted for human trafficking and murder, client of Griffen + Smoltz
Jim, Agent, U.S. Secret Service
John Arnold, father of Detective AJ Arnold
Brenda Arnold, mother of Detective AJ Arnold
Isabella Rios, U.S. Department of Agriculture employee, stabbed to death in *Fatal Frenzy*
Deborah Gainsville, mother of two, stabbed to death in *Fatal Frenzy*

Barry Scanlon, bartender, stabbing victim who survived in *Fatal Frenzy*

Tara, Public Affairs Officer, Metro PD

**Jesse Best, U.S. Marshal

**Marcus, Sam's favorite designer from Virginia

Jim Rollins, Head of Security, JW Marriott

Mindy Cahill, student at Northern Connecticut University, kidnapped in *Fatal Frenzy*

Jennifer Torlino, student at Northern Connecticut University, kidnapped in *Fatal Frenzy*

Debbie McLane, faculty chaperone, Northern Connecticut University

Brian Watkins, student, Northern Connecticut University

Tyler Johnston, student, Northern Connecticut University

Wednesday Alexander, known as "Wendy," student, Northern Connecticut University

Joe Warren, Owner, McDuffy's bar

Vanessa Christie, Bartender, McDuffy's bar

Book 10:
Fatal Identity

Released: August 1, 2016

Back cover copy:

Every family has its secrets...

As the first anniversary of her marriage to Vice President Nick Cappuano approaches, Lieutenant Sam Holland is dreaming of Bora Bora—sun, sand and a desperately needed break from the DC grind. But real life has a way of intervening, and Sam soon finds herself taking on one of the most perplexing cases of her career.

Government worker Josh Hamilton begs Sam to investigate his shocking claim that his parents stole him from another family thirty years ago. More complicated still, his "father" is none other than the FBI director. When a member of Josh's family is brutally murdered, Sam begins to question how deep the cover-up goes. Is it possible the revered director was part of a baby-napping ring and others involved are also targets? With a killer intent on deadly revenge and her team still reeling from a devastating loss, Sam's plate is full—and when Nick and their son, Scotty, take ill, is her dream of a tropical anniversary celebration in peril, too?

More about the story...

Sam and Nick are getting ready to celebrate their first anniversary in Bora Bora, but they have some unfinished business to attend to before they leave. Sam is suspended for three days for punching Ramsey and faces the possibility of being charged. Nick and Scotty are sick with the flu.

After seeing an age-progressed photo that looks just like him, Josh Hamilton, the son of FBI Director Troy Hamilton, believes he was kidnapped as a baby 30 years ago from Tennessee. Sam and Avery investigate the case.

U.S. Attorney Tom Forrester sends Sam's assault case to the grand jury and will abide by their decision of whether or not to charge her.

Director Hamilton is murdered in his home, and Avery finds the body. Freddie puts Josh in a safe place until they know what's going on as the case takes Sam to Tennessee, where she comes down with the flu as well.

Sam gives her first speech as Second Lady and repairs a twenty-year rift with her mother, Brenda.

Characters

Recurring Marked with **
** Samantha "Sam" Holland Cappuano, Lieutenant, Commander, Homicide Division, Metro PD
**Nicholas "Nick" Cappuano, Vice President of the United States

Leslie Monroe, Executive Assistant Director for Criminal, Cyber, Response and Services Branch, Federal Bureau of Investigation
Dustin Jacoby, Deputy Director, Federal Bureau of Investigation
Courtney Hamilton, wife of FBI Director Troy Hamilton
Josh Hamilton, son of FBI Director Troy Hamilton
Gillian MacKenzie, Associate Deputy Director, Federal Bureau of Investigation
Danielle Koch, Receptionist, Knoxville Field Office, Federal Bureau of Investigation
Dale Owens, Agent, Knoxville Field Office, Federal Bureau of Investigation
Mildred Spires, former Hamilton family neighbor, Knoxville, TN
Mark Hamilton, son of FBI Director Troy Hamilton
Maura Hamilton, daughter of FBI Director Troy Hamilton
Nancy Dumphries, friend of Courtney Hamilton in Knoxville
Chris Kinney, witness
**Nate, Agent on VP Detail, U.S. Secret Service

Chauncey Rollings, father to Taylor Rollings, kidnapped as an infant
Micki Rollings, mother to Taylor Rollings, kidnapped as an infant
Kurt Hager, Criminal Defense Attorney, representing Sam
Watson, Detective, Franklin County, Tennessee Police Department

Book 11: Fatal Threat

Released: July 25, 2017

Back cover copy:

With a killer on the loose, it's the worst time to be on lockdown...

It's another day at the office for Washington Metro Police Lieutenant Sam Holland when a body surfaces off the shores of the Anacostia River. Before Sam can sink her teeth into the new case, Secret Service agents seize her from the crime scene. A threat has been made against her family, and nobody will tell her anything—including the whereabouts of her husband, Vice President Nick Cappuano. This isn't the first time the couple's lives have been at risk, but when a bombshell from Sam's past returns to haunt her, she can't help but wonder if there's a connection. With a ruthless killer out for vengeance, and Nick struggling to maintain his reputation after secrets from his own past are revealed, Sam tries to tie the threat to a murder that can't possibly be a coincidence. And she has to get it done before her husband's career is irrevocably damaged…

More about the story…

Sam and Freddie are investigating a body found in the Anacostia River. The Secret Service suddenly appears, grabs Sam and takes her to the bunker along with the rest of the family after a credible threat was received while Nick is out of the country on official business. The Metro PD, uncertain whether Sam has been kidnapped, investigate the situation.

Sam's ex-husband, Peter Gibson, is tortured and murdered, which sends Sam into an unexpected spiral of grief when it becomes clear he protected her from whomever has threatened their family. Nick's mother, Nicoletta, gives an interview full of lies about him.

Shelby gives birth to Noah and breaks up with Avery after he says Sam's name in the throes of passion. Jeannie and Michael get married. Sam meets Fairfax Detective Cameron Green and encourages him to apply for the opening on her team left by the death of Detective Arnold. Gonzo continues to grapple with complex grief over his partner's murder.

The investigation leads to a most unexpected suspect and puts Sam and Nick in an awkward situation as they try to decide how to proceed.

Characters

Recurring Marked with **
** Samantha "Sam" Holland Cappuano, Lieutenant, Commander, Homicide Division, Metro PD
**Nicholas "Nick" Cappuano, Vice President of the United States

**Brendan Sullivan, Parole Officer, District of Columbia
Mike Lonergan, witness, works at Navy Yard
Ruby Denton, student, Capitol University, missing in *Fatal Identity*
Thomas J. Jackson, Agent, U.S. Secret Service
Daniel Cooley, Agent, U.S. Secret Service
Irma Gibson, mother of Peter Gibson
Donny Bautista, Entrepreneur, friend of Peter Gibson
Lucy Kaul, coworker and girlfriend of Peter Gibson
Dwayne Rogers, friend of Peter Gibson
Anton Williams, works at District Market
Rose Samuels, prostitute and drug addict, found floating in Anacostia River in *Fatal Threat*
Amber Dillon, Reporter, CBC
Marilyn, Irma Gibson's friend
Amelia, high school girlfriend of Nick's who died of leukemia
Adele Jacobs, neighbor of Lucy Kaul
Buzz Janson, Founder of Politician.com gossip site
**Noah Faircloth Hill, son of Shelby Faircloth , later adopted by Avery Hill
Dante Fields, friend of Peter's
**Christopher Nelson, son of President David Nelson and First Lady Gloria Nelson

Stanley Ritter, Aide to Christopher Nelson
**Cameron Green, Detective, Fairfax County, later Homicide Division, MPD
Phil Kent, worked with Peter Gibson
James, Detective, Partner to Cameron Green, Fairfax County

Book 12:
Fatal Chaos

Released: February 27, 2018

Back cover copy:

First the calm. Then the storm…

Escaping D.C. during the dog days of summer is one of the smartest moves Washington Metro Police Lieutenant Sam Holland ever made. Beach walks aren't quite as romantic with the Secret Service in tow, but Sam and her husband, Vice President Nick Cappuano, cherish the chance to recharge and reconnect—especially with a scandal swirling around the administration. No sooner are they back home than a fatal drive-by shooting sets the city on edge. The teenage victim is barely older than Sam and Nick's son, Scotty. As more deaths follow, Sam and her team play beat the clock to stop the ruthless killers. With Nick facing his greatest challenge—one that could drastically change all their lives and even end Sam's career—will the mounting pressure deepen or damage their bond?

More about the story...

Sam and Nick are trying to cope with learning that President Nelson's son was the one who threatened their family and killed Sam's ex-husband. Press coverage of the situation is relentless and has raised their already high profile to dangerous levels. As they are returning from vacation, a string of fatal drive-by shootings terrorizes the District.

Sam and Gonzo tease Freddie about his upcoming bachelor party, which Sam is hosting. Detective Cameron Green joins the Metro PD Homicide Division as Gonzo's new partner and finds that Arnold's big shoes are hard to fill. Shelby and Avery make up.

Deputy Chief Conklin is suspended for three days after hiding that a former member of the Metro PD is missing while conducting his own investigation.

A retired Metro PD sharpshooter, who has been missing during the drive-by shooting spree, is the prime suspect. Sam is punched in the face by a SWAT officer after she uncovers his affair during the investigation and reports the findings to her superiors, ending the officer's marriage in the process.

Nick is being pressured to testify against Nelson in front of Congress about the situation with Nelson's son.

Characters

Recurring Marked with **

** Samantha "Sam" Holland Cappuano, Lieutenant, Commander, Homicide Division, Metro PD
**Nicholas "Nick" Cappuano, Vice President of the United States

Danita Jackson, mother of shooting victim Jamal Jackson
Jamal Jackson, teenager, murdered in *Fatal Chaos*
Misty Jackson, sister of Jamal Jackson
Tamara Jackson, sister of Jamal Jackson
Vincent Andina, friend of Jamal Jackson
David Richie, friend of Jamal Jackson
Melinda Kramer, expectant mother, murdered in *Fatal Chaos*
Joe Kramer, husband of Melinda Kramer
Sarah Kramer, sister of Joe Kramer
Kelsey, witness to shooting
Charlie, witness to shooting
Sridhar Kapoor, doctoral student at Georgetown University, murdered in *Fatal Chaos*
Rayna Kapoor, wife of Sridhar Kapoor
Caroline Brinkley, murdered in *Fatal Chaos*
Vanessa Marchand, six-year-old, murdered in *Fatal Chaos*
**Trey Marchand, Vanessa's father
Delilah, Caroline Brinkley's roommate
Jian Chang, nurse, murdered in *Fatal Chaos*
Mary Jane Demmers, interviewed in investigation
Rod Demmers, interviewed in investigation
**Keeney, Officer, Patrol Division, Metro PD

Dr. Rosemary Merrill, Psychiatrist treating Avery Hill
**Kenneth Wallack, Sharpshooter (retired), Metro PD, peer of Skip Holland, Joe Farnsworth, Jake Malone
Fitzgivens, Sharpshooter, SWAT Division, Metro PD
Sellers, Sharpshooter, SWAT Division, Metro PD
**Sgt. Dylan Offenbach, Sharpshooter, SWAT Division, Metro PD
Ginger, Shelby's sister

Book 13: Fatal Invasion

Released: November 27, 2018

Back cover copy:

First the fire, then the heat…

A brutal home invasion. Two small, traumatized survivors who may have witnessed the horror. Lieutenant Sam Holland has never worked a case quite like this one, in which her eye-witnesses are five-year-old twins. But when Sam steps up in a big way for them, she risks her heart as much as her career. While Sam and her husband, Vice President Nick Cappuano, go to battle in more ways than one for her tiny witnesses, her colleague Sergeant Tommy "Gonzo" Gonzales battles his own demons. Months of unbearable grief and despair come to a head in an unimaginable way that threatens Gonzo's status with the department and his relationship with his fiancée, Christina. With trouble both at Metro PD headquarters and on the case, Sam struggles to keep her priorities straight at home and at work while trying not to lose her heart to her latest crime victims.

More about the story...

We meet Aubrey and Alden Armstrong after their parents are killed in a tragic home invasion and fire. The investigation quickly focuses on the business partner that threatened to kill Jameson Armstrong and forced the family into hiding. Nick is preparing for a trip to Europe and wants Sam to go with him. Alex is sick, and Gonzo is missing because he's high on pills. He ends up in rehab.

Elin and Freddie get married at the Naval Observatory, the official residence of the Vice President. Sam and Nick become guardians to Alden and Aubrey. We are introduced to Elijah, Alden and Aubrey's older brother and guardian, who agrees to let Sam and Nick to care for the twins, who they begin to refer to as "The Littles." Their late mother's sister wants custody, too, but Elijah chooses to leave the children with the Cappuanos. Dr. Harry Flynn and Sam's chief of staff, Lilia Von Nostrand go public as a couple.

Characters

Recurring Marked with **
** Samantha "Sam" Holland Cappuano, Lieutenant, Commander, Homicide Division, Metro PD

Nicholas "Nick" Cappuano, Vice President of the United States

Jameson Armstrong, (also known as Griffin Beauclair) husband of Cleo, father of Elijah, Aubrey and Alden, victim of home invasion/fire, deceased in *Fatal Invasion*

Cleo Armstrong (Beauclair), wife of Jameson, mother of Aubrey and Alden, victim of home invasion/fire, murdered in *Fatal Invasion*

**Aubrey Armstrong (Beauclair), daughter of Jameson and Cleo

**Alden Armstrong (Beauclair), son of Jameson and Cleo

**Elijah Armstrong (Beauclair), son of Jameson and his ex-wife Margaret Armstrong, and brother to Aubrey and Alden

Duke Piermont, Jameson's former business partner

Dave Gorton, Jameson's former business partner

Mrs. Wallace, Social Worker, George Washington University Hospital

Beatrice Reeve, director of Armstrong children's school

Lauren Morton, neighbor of Armstrong family

Janice McMillian, neighbor of Armstrong family

**Dolores Finklestein, social worker, Child and Family Services, District of Columbia

Margaret Armstrong, Jameson's first wife, mother of Elijah

Jameson's former company

Marlene Peters, witness

Emma Knoff, President of the Parent Teacher Organization at Northwest Academy

****Monique Lawson,** Cleo's sister and aunt to Alden and Aubrey

****Robert Lawson,** Monique's husband

****Leslie Dennis,** Cleo's mother, grandmother to Alden and Aubrey

****Chad Dennis,** Cleo's father, grandfather to Alden and Aubrey

Victor Klein, suspect

Alden Jenkins, friend of Klein's

Danny Baker, friend of Klein's

Luisa Sanchez, housekeeper in neighborhood

****Milagros Cortez,** housekeeper to Armstrong family

Book 14:
Fatal
Reckoning

Released: March 26, 2019

Back cover copy:

When tragedy strikes, a cold case suddenly turns hot—and deadly.

A peaceful morning is shattered when Washington Metro Police Lieutenant Sam Holland's beloved father succumbs to injuries from an unsolved shooting while on duty four years ago. As the community rallies around Sam and her family, one thing becomes crystal clear: her father's death has turned the unsolved case into a homicide—and it's on her to bring her father's killer to justice. But the case has been cold for years…until an anonymous tip that's too shocking to believe leads Sam down a dark and dangerous path. Her husband, Vice President Nick Cappuano, knows if she can't solve this case, it will haunt her for the rest of her life. She'll need the strength of their bond to pull her out of the darkness before it's too late, because as the missing pieces rapidly fall into place, Sam realizes the truth might just break her all the same—and that her father's killer isn't done yet…

More about the story…

A frantic call from her stepmother leads to one of Sam's worst nightmares come true—the death of her beloved father, Skip. Sam is forced to make the unimaginable decision to let him go rather than allow EMTs to resuscitate him, which angers her beloved stepmother, Celia. Nick is on his way home from Europe when he learns of Skip's death. Freddie and Elin are on their honeymoon in Italy and he makes the decision to come home to be with Sam and their family.

As a police funeral is planned for Skip, Sam and her squad begin a reinvigorated investigation into his shooting, which has now been upgraded to homicide. Sam and Freddie find a connection between Skip's case and the long unsolved murder of his first partner, Steven Coyne.

Shock reverberates through the department when it's learned that a close friend of Skip's had information about his shooting that he kept secret for years.

DEA Agent Patrick Connolly is hit and killed by a stray bullet while walking on 12th Street at lunchtime. Darren Tabor introduces Sam to Roni Connolly, his colleague at the Washington *Star*. Sam has to give Roni the dreadful news about her husband's death and feels an immediate affinity for the young woman.

Angela, Sam's sister, is pregnant with her third child.

Characters

Recurring Marked with **
** **Samantha "Sam" Holland Cappuano,** Lieutenant, Commander, Homicide Division, Metro PD
**Nicholas "Nick" Cappuano, Vice President of the United States

**Neveah Charles, Officer, Metro PD, liaison to Holland family for planning of Skip's funeral
Roy Gallagher, City Councilman, District of Columbia
Mick Santoro, Associate of Gallagher's
Dermott Ryan, Owner, O'Leary's Pub, Associate of Gallagher's
**Veronica "Roni" Connolly, obituary writer, Washington *Star*, wife of murdered DEA Agent Patrick Connolly
Patrick Connolly, Agent, Drug Enforcement Agency, husband of Roni, murdered in *Fatal Reckoning*

Book 15:
Fatal
Accusation

Released: December 17, 2019

Back cover copy:

A deadly serious affair…

The story breaks as Metro PD Lieutenant Sam Holland attends a dinner party with her husband, Vice President Nick Cappuano: President Nelson is accused of having an affair. More shocking still, campaign staffer Tara Weber claims the president fathered her newborn son—while the First Lady was undergoing secret cancer treatment. When a high-profile murder case hits Sam's desk, she's shocked to uncover a connection to the presidential scandal. With the department caught up in its own internal scandals, and the chief's job hanging by a thread, Sam questions who she can trust as her team uncovers information that clouds an already-murky case. And with calls for the president to resign getting louder by the minute, Sam needs to close this case before she finds herself living at 1600 Pennsylvania Avenue.

More about the story…

Tara Weber, an employee of the Nelson campaign, claims that President Nelson is the father of her baby. After the story breaks, Tara is found murdered. Sam and Nick are in a race against the clock to solve the case, so they aren't forced to move to the White House if Nelson has to resign, especially after learning that Gloria Nelson was battling ovarian cancer while her husband was having an affair.

A reporter asks them when they're going to have "real" children, even though they adopted Scotty, and are guardians to the "Littles." The question is deeply offensive to the Cappuanos.

Sam breaks her flip phone and is relieved to get a new one. Sam and Dr. Trulo create a grief group for victims of violent crime. Shelby and Avery get married, Avery adopts Noah, and Shelby is pregnant.

Characters

Recurring Marked with **

** **Samantha "Sam" Holland Cappuano,** Lieutenant, Commander, Homicide Division, Metro PD

****Nicholas "Nick" Cappuano,** Vice President of the United States

Tara Weber, senior policy advisor to the president during the Nelson Campaign, had affair with the president, mother of infant son

****Clare,** Officer, Patrol Division, Metro PD

****Youncy,** Officer, Patrol Division, Metro PD

Delany Russo, Tara's assistant

Ben, Tara's cousin

Charles Weber, Tara's father

Diana Weber, Tara's mother

Bryce Massey, Tara's ex-boyfriend

Isabel, Intern, World Bank

Paige Thompson, Tara's former business partner

Roland Dunning, Defense Attorney for Conklin

Carly Sargant, Friend of Tara

Suzanne King, Friend of Tara

Ben Wilton, Congressman and boyfriend of Tara

Tim Finley, Editor/CEO, DailyPolitic

****Monica,** Shelby's sister

Davis Faircloth, Shelby's father

Josh Hill, Avery's brother

Robert Mercer, Agent, U.S. Secret Service, Nelson detail

Olivia Jenson, Agent, U.S. Secret Service, Nelson detail

Hank Reynolds, Agent, U.S. Secret Service, Nelson detail

Book 16:
Fatal Fraud

Released: November 20, 2020

Back cover copy:

A dangerous truth revealed…

A prominent member of the D.C. community has been murdered, pulling Lieutenant Sam Holland into yet another high-stakes homicide investigation that has her trying to connect the dots between a dead woman and the friends and family who'd turned against her right before her untimely death. With numerous scandals still fresh within the department's ranks, Sam is under more than the usual amount of pressure on the job. All the while, Sam's husband, Vice President Nick Cappuano, faces mounting calls to declare his intention to run for president in the coming election, leaving the second couple feeling the strain at home—and on the job as the family endures the first holidays without their beloved patriarch, Skip Holland. As always, when things become too hot to handle on the job, Sam and Nick turn to each other for solace in the storm.

More about the story...

The week before Thanksgiving, Sam, Nick, Freddie, Elin, Michael, and Jeannie go visit Gonzo in rehab in Baltimore. Nick announces that he's not running for president in the next election. He wants to be home with the family he's yearned for all his life. Sam and Trulo's grief group meets for the first time.

Sam discovers that Virginia McLeod's husband and daughter were involved in the fraud.

Freddie is held at gunpoint by one of Virginia McLeod's fraud victims.

Gonzo and Christina get married on Thanksgiving night. Later, Sam and Nick are relaxing in bed after a full day when he gets a call on the emergency phone line from the White House that will change their lives forever.

Sam and Nick's story continues in an all-new series, beginning with STATE OF AFFAIRS!

Characters

Recurring Marked with **
** Samantha "Sam" Holland Cappuano, Lieutenant, Commander, Homicide Division, Metro PD
**Nicholas "Nick" Cappuano, Vice President of the United States

Henry, Agent, U.S. Secret Service, Cappuano detail
Virginia 'Ginny' McLeod, defrauded friends, murder victim in *Fatal Fraud*
Kenneth McLeod, husband of Ginny
**Phillips, Officer, Patrol Division, Metro PD
**Jestings, Officer, Patrol Division, Metro PD
Dan and Toni Alino, friends of McLeod's, defrauded by Ginny
Brett Haverson, tipped off the FBI about Ginny after being defrauded by her
Clarissa Haverson, Brett's wife
Amy Turnblat, Executive Chef, La Belle Vie in Potomac, Ramsey's extramarital lover
**Lenore Worthington, mother of cold case murder victim Calvin Worthington
**Calvin Worthington, murdered as a teenager fifteen years ago
Alison Enders, Ginny's cousin
Tanya, Receptionist, Office of the Vice President of the United States
Mandi McLeod, daughter of Ginny and Ken
Kenneth McLeod Jr., son of Ginny and Ken
Kayla Owen, Reporter at WKLA-TV, asked the "real children" question

Cheri Clark, Realtor who worked with Ginny
**Vernon, Agent, U.S. Secret Service, assigned to Sam
**Jimmy, Agent, U.S. Secret Service, assigned to Sam
Mark Townsend, Owner, VocalExchange Recording Studio
Rob Heinke, Engineer, VocalExchange
Tina Goss, College friend of Ginny's who invested with her
Jack Goss, Tina's husband who died by suicide
Celeste, friend of Tina's
Valerie Southern, student who Sam rescues on the Metro
Hattie Townsend, Mark Townsend's wife
Clara, older woman in Gonzo's building who watches Alex
Kourtney, Agent, U.S. Secret Service, assigned to Sam
Belinda, Agent, U.S. Secret Service, assigned to Sam
Janet Milton, sister of Ginny McLeod
Baker, Officer, Patrol Division, Metro PD

About the Author

Marie Force is the *New York Times* bestselling author of more than 100 contemporary romance, romantic suspense and erotic romance novels. Her series include Fatal, First Family, Gansett Island, Butler Vermont, Quantum, Treading Water, Miami Nights and Wild Widows. She has also written 12 single titles, with more coming.

Her books have sold more than 14 million copies worldwide, have been translated into more than a dozen languages and have appeared on the *New York Times* bestseller list more than 30 times. She is also a *USA Today* and #1 *Wall Street Journal* bestseller, as well as a Spiegel bestseller in Germany.

Her goals in life are simple—to spend as much time as possible with her young adult children, to keep writing books for as long as she possibly can and to never be on a flight that makes the news.

Join Marie's mailing list on her website at marieforce.com for news about new books and upcoming appearances in your area. Follow her on Facebook at www.facebook.com/MarieForceAuthor, Instagram at www.instagram.com/marieforceauthor and TikTok at www.tiktok.com/@marieforceauthor?. Contact Marie at marie@marieforce.com.

Made in the USA
Monee, IL
18 June 2025

19585942R10069